Stephanie's Ponytail

Story by Robert Munsch

Art by Michael Martchenko

Annick Press Ltd. • Toronto • New York

One day Stephanie went to her mom and said, "None of the kids in my class have a ponytail. I want a nice ponytail coming right out the back."

So Stephanie's mom gave her a nice ponytail coming right out the back.

When Stephanie went to school the other kids looked at her and said, "Ugly, ugly, *very* ugly."

Stephanie said, "It's *my ponytail* and *I* like it."

The next morning, when Stephanie went to school, all the other girls had ponytails coming out the back.

Stephanie looked at them and said, "You are all a bunch of copycats. You just do whatever I do. You don't have a brain in your heads."

The next morning the mom said, "Stephanie, would you like a ponytail coming out the back?"

Stephanie said, "No."

"Then that's that," said her mom. "That's the only place you can do ponytails."

"No, it's not," said Stephanie. "I want one coming out the side, just above my ear."

"Very strange," said the mom. "Are you sure that is what you want?"

"Yes," said Stephanie.

So her mom gave Stephanie a nice ponytail coming out right above her ear.

When she went to school the other kids saw her and said, "Ugly, ugly, *very* ugly."

Stephanie said, "It's *my ponytail* and *I* like it."

The next morning when Stephanie came to school all the girls, and even some of the boys, had nice ponytails coming out just above their ears.

The next morning the mom said, "Stephanie, would you like a ponytail coming out the back?"

Stephanie said, "NNNO."

"Would you like one coming out the side?"

"NNNO!"

"Then that's that," said her mom. "There is no other place you can do ponytails."

"Yes, there is," said Stephanie. "I want one coming out of the top of my head like a tree."

"That's very, very strange," said her mom. "Are you sure that is what you want?"

"Yes," said Stephanie.

So her mom gave Stephanie a nice ponytail coming out of the top of her head like a tree. When Stephanie went to school, the other kids saw her and said, "Ugly, ugly, *very* ugly."

Stephanie said, "It's *my ponytail* and *I* like it."

The next day all of the girls and all of the boys had pony- tails coming out the top. It looked like broccoli was growing out of their heads.

The next morning the mom said, "Stephanie, would you like a ponytail coming out the back?"

Stephanie said, "NNNO."

"Would you like one coming out the side?"

"NNNO!"

"Would you like one coming out the top?"

"NNNO!"

"Then that is definitely that," said the mom. "There is no other place you can do ponytails."

"Yes, there is," said Stephanie. "I want one coming out the front and hanging down in front of my nose."

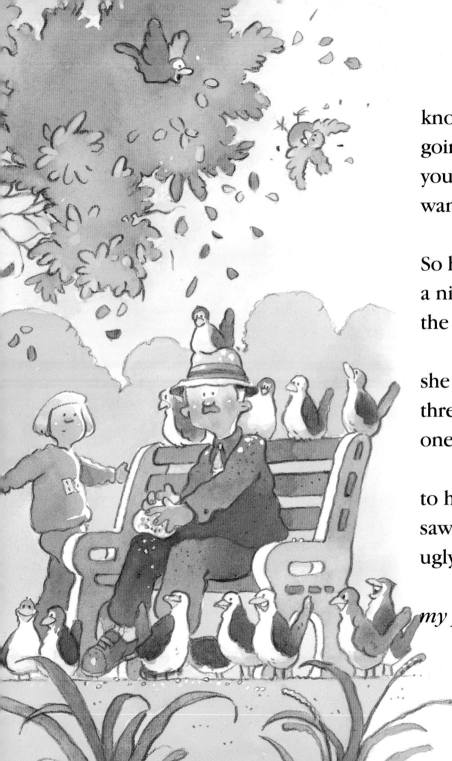

"But nobody will know if you are coming or going," her mom said. "Are you sure that is what you want?"

"Yes," said Stephanie. So her mom gave Stephanie a nice ponytail coming out the front.

On the way to school she bumped into four trees, three cars, two houses and one Principal.

When she finally got to her class the other kids saw her and said, "Ugly, ugly, *very* ugly."

Stephanie said, "It's *my ponytail* and *I* like it."

The next day all of the girls and all of the boys, and even the teacher, had ponytails coming out the front and hanging down in front of their noses. None of them could see where they were going. They bumped into the desks and they bumped into each other. They bumped into the walls, and, by mistake, three girls went into the boys' bathroom.

Stephanie yelled, "You are a bunch of brainless copycats. You just do whatever I do. When I come tomorrow I am going to have...SHAVED MY HEAD!"

The first person to come the next day was the teacher. She had shaved her head and she was bald.

The next to come were the boys. They had shaved their heads and they were bald.

The next to come were the girls. They had shaved their heads and they were bald.

The last person to come was Stephanie, and she had...

a nice little ponytail coming right out the back.

Annick Press gratefully acknowledges the support of the Canada Council
and the Ontario Arts Council.

Canadian Cataloguing in Publication Data
    Munsch, Robert N., 1945–
        Stephanie's ponytail

    (Munsch for kids)
    ISBN 1-55037-485-0 (bound)   ISBN 1-55037-484-2 (pbk.)

    I. Martchenko, Michael. II. Title. III. Title:
    Robert N., 1945–   . Munsch for kids.

    PS8576.U575S74 1996   jC813'.54   C96-930149-9
    PZ7.M85St 1996

The art in this book was rendered in watercolours.
The text was typeset in Garamond.

Distributed in Canada by: Published in the U.S.A. by Annick Press (U.S.) Ltd.
Firefly Books Ltd.   Distributed in the U.S.A. by:
3680 Victoria Park Avenue   Firefly Books (U.S.) Inc.
Willowdale, ON   P.O. Box 1338
M2H 3K1   Ellicott Station
                                   Buffalo, NY 14205

Printed and bound in Canada by Metropole Litho, Montreal

To Stephanie Caswell, Durham, Ontario
                                        – Bob Munsch